Pumpkin Town!

(Or, Nothing Is Better and Worse Than Pumpkins)

written by **Katie McKy**   illustrated by **Pablo Bernasconi**

CLARION BOOKS
An Imprint OF HARPERCOLLINS*Publishers*
BOSTON NEW YORK

José and his family grew pumpkins. That growing began with shiny seeds, which were followed by long vines, and those vines grew every which way.

The pumpkins grew every which way too, from small to fat and tall.

The Jack-Be-Littles could be dropped into pockets.

The Happy Jacks were bigger: a strong enough boy could carry just one.

The Big Moons were bigger still: too large for five boys to roll.

Come fall, José and his family would gather the pumpkins and collect the vines. Then two trucks took the fruit to faraway cities. Some were hollowed and carved and some were saved for pies.

But before the trucks took the pumpkins, José and his family saved a few. They needed the seeds.

When it came to saving pumpkins, José's father always said: "Save only the best and sell the rest!"

So José and his brothers hollowed the best pumpkins and saved only the biggest, brightest seeds.

They took the duller, smaller seeds to the edge of
the field overlooking the town and tossed them.

But one gusty, dusty October day, when José and his
brothers took the lesser seeds to the edge of the field
and flung them, the wind caught those seeds and carried
them and didn't let them loose until they fell like rain
down on the distant town.

The seeds slipped into straw roofs and settled into
flowerpots and sprinkled gardens.

And that seemed to be the end of it.

But the next spring, rain awoke those small seeds, and plants began.

More rain fell and vines grew every which way. They wrapped around chimneys and wound through corn.

At first, the townspeople liked the vines, for they were lovely and delicate.

But then the vines began to climb, up and down and around, growing leafy and thick. They snaked green and silent through one window and then out another.

Then fruit grew. And grew... and grew, every which way.

Soon, the townspeople were stepping over pumpkins and around pumpkins and under pumpkins; it was hard to walk even a block.

Rooftops sagged under the weight of Big Moons. Fences fell, and when the wind blew one had to dodge Happy Jacks and Jack-Be-Littles falling from trees.

"Nothing is worse than pumpkins!" groaned the townspeople.

Meanwhile, up on their mountainside, José and his family cut and stacked their pumpkins, saving only the best, and when they were done, they stepped back and said: "Nothing is better than pumpkins!"

But when José and his family looked down at the town, it looked odd. It seemed so green. And orange...

Since their fieldwork was done, and because José and his brothers were curious, they walked to town the next day, where they saw more vines and pumpkins than they'd ever imagined.

They remembered the gusty, dusty day that they'd scattered the seeds.

"It is our fault," whispered José.

"We must do something," whispered his brothers.

"We rest for now," whispered José.

But that night, José and his brothers cut and stacked the pumpkins
and vines. They worked as quietly as they could, but some townspeople
still sneaked peeks. They marveled at how well the brothers worked.

The brothers climbed up poles and twined through trees
and snaked silent through one window and out another,
gathering and stacking pumpkins and vines.

When the townspeople awoke,
they discovered a mountain of
pumpkins and a hill of vines and
a mound of tired brothers.

While the brothers slept, the townspeople filled a wagon with hay and set five great watermelons between José and his brothers, in thanks for their aid. That wagon took the brothers back to their home, where they were laid in the glossy grass, still sleeping.

When their father found them there, he asked them what they had
done to deserve the great watermelons.

"We just helped the townspeople with their harvest," the brothers
said, which was true, and nothing more was said.

Down in the town, five trucks came for the mountain of pumpkins, and the townspeople were given a grand sum of money for all that fruit.

"Ahhh, nothing is better than pumpkins," they said.

Much of the money went toward a feast, held around a bonfire made by burning the hill of vines. It was decided then that the rest of the pumpkin money would be spent to carve a statue, a statue of the five mysterious brothers who had made a mountain of pumpkins.

It took all of the next week for the townspeople to repair their roofs and their fences, and it took all of that week for José and his brothers and his father to eat their great gifts.

The melons were so sweet that José and his family said: "Nothing is better than watermelons!"

"Be careful with the seeds," José's father said. "Our field grows pumpkins, not watermelons."

So José's family filled a great bowl with seeds, and those seeds were forgotten . . . until a day later, when the wind roused José's father at night.

He feared that some of those watermelon seeds might be blown into their field.

By moonlight, he carried the bowl to the edge of his field and he tossed the seeds.

The wind caught those seeds and carried them and didn't let them loose until they fell like rain down on the town.

The watermelon seeds slipped into straw roofs and settled into flowerpots and sprinkled gardens and slid into the soil around the statue of José and his brothers.

And that seemed to be the end of it.

For Mick, who girds all my words —K. M.

For Natalia, seed of my inspiration —P. B.

Text copyright © 2006 by Katie McKy
Illustrations copyright © 2006 by Pablo Bernasconi

Clarion Books and the Clarion Books logo are trademarks of HarperCollins Publishers LLC.

clarionbooks.com

The text of this book is set in 20-point Mrs. Eaves Roman.
The illustrations are collaged original art and found objects.

Library of Congress Cataloging-in-Publication Data
McKy, Katie.
  Pumpkin town! or, Nothing is better and worse than pumpkins / written by Katie McKy and
illustrated by Pablo Bernasconi.
    p. cm.
  title: Nothing is better and worse than pumpkins.
  Summary: Once, after a bountiful pumpkin harvest, as five brothers dispose of unneeded seeds, the seeds
suddenly go flying with the wind and cover the town below, but the brothers think nothing more about it.
  HC ISBN-13: 978-0-618-60569-9 PA ISBN-13: 978-0-547-18193-6
[1. Pumpkin—Fiction. 2. Brothers—Fiction.] I. Title: Nothing is better and worse than pumpkins.
II. Bernasconi, Pablo, 1973– ill. III. Title.
  PZ7.M4786957Pum 2006   [E]—dc22   2005003918

Manufactured in China
LEO 20 19 18 17 16
4500845149